BIG JEREMY

For Norma Klein

S.K.

Text copyright © 1989 by Steven Kroll
Illustrations copyright © 1989 by Donald Carrick
Printed in the United States of America
First Edition

Library of Congress Cataloging-in-Publication Data

Kroll, Steven.
Big Jeremy.

Summary: When his clumsiness causes problems for his
small neighbors, Jeremy, a friendly giant, decides to
run away.
[1. Giants—Fiction]   I. Carrick, Donald, ill.
II. Title.
PZ7.K9225Bjm   1989   [E]   88-35812
ISBN 0-8234-0759-4

BIG JEREMY

Steven Kroll

illustrated by

Donald Carrick

Holiday House/New York

Big Jeremy was a giant. He lived in an enormous barn on the bank of a river at the edge of an apple orchard in Maine. Every morning, he read the paper in his big, comfortable chair, which was the size of an elephant. Every night, he slept in his big bed, which was as long as a tennis court. In the evenings, he loved watching the sun set over Terison's Orchard.

Jeremy worked every day in the orchard. When Elwood and Sal Terison and their seven sons and daughters-in-law and all their grandchildren saw him coming, they'd shout, "Good morning, Jeremy!"

Then Big Jeremy would give the children rides on his shoulders. Afterwards, he'd help Elwood and Sal and their seven sons and daughters-in-law with their chores.

He built Sal a cider mill in half a day.

He plowed Roger Terison's fields with his giant hoe and was done in half an hour.

In the autumn, he picked all the apples in the orchard.

Each evening when Jeremy finished work, the Terisons gave him a big bag of food. He carried it over to his barn and cooked his dinner on a stove as big as a grizzly bear. His favorite meal was two dozen hamburgers, four roast chickens, fifty-six carrots, five big bowls of spaghetti, twenty-five scoops of mashed potatoes, and seven chocolate cakes. When he was finished eating, he watched the sunset.

Jeremy's life in the orchard was very peaceful. Then, quite suddenly, everything started going wrong.

It was a summer evening. Jeremy was dozing when he heard the cry from the big house where Elwood and Sal and their seven sons and daughters-in-law and all their grandchildren lived together.

"Fire!" someone shouted. "Fire!"

Jeremy opened his eyes. Flames were beginning to rise in the orchard.

Quickly Big Jeremy started toward the blaze. When he reached the orchard, the Terisons' seven sons and daughters-in-law and all their grandchildren were throwing water at the burning trees. Elwood and Sal were in the house, filling buckets at the kitchen sink. They were passing them out the door as fast as they could.

"Jeremy, you've got to help us!" cried Roger.

Jeremy took a deep breath and let it go. Instantly the fire went out. At the same moment, the seven Terison sons and daughters-in-law and all the grandchildren were blown out of sight!

Elwood and Sal couldn't believe what they'd just seen. They stood speechless at the kitchen door.

Then they started running around.

"Our children!" shouted Elwood.

"Our grandchildren!" shouted Sal.

"I'll find them!" shouted Jeremy. "Don't worry, I'll bring them back!"

He rushed off into the night, leaping over apple trees.

He reached the river and began to wade across. But it was very dark, and he couldn't see where he was going. CRASH! He put his foot right through the bridge.

Jeremy stood in the water, wondering what to do. Then he heard shouts from the far shore. It was the Terisons' seven sons and daughters-in-law and all their grandchildren. They'd found their way home already!

"Thank goodness," said Jeremy. "I'd better help them."

He stretched himself between the two shores, and the Terisons' seven sons and daughters-in-law and all their grandchildren began hurrying across the river on his back. As they reached his neck, their feet began to tickle him. Jeremy lost his grip.

KERPLASH! He fell into the water. The Terisons' seven sons and daughters-in-law and all their grandchildren fell in, too.

Everyone splashed and sputtered. Finally Roger Terison shouted, "Jeremy, get us out of here!"

Jeremy helped everyone out of the water. Then he went back to
his barn and plopped down in his chair.

He was sad. He couldn't seem to do anything right. Maybe the
Terisons would be better off without him.

The next day, everything seemed gloomy. It wasn't even fun fixing the bridge. All Jeremy could think about was how clumsy he'd been.

That night, when everyone was asleep, Jeremy sneaked out of his barn. He built a raft and floated away down the river.

By morning he was far from home. When he stopped at a village for food, the villagers got so scared, they ran away!

For many months, Big Jeremy wandered, living as best he could on roots and berries. When the weather was good, he slept under the stars. When it was bad, he huddled in a forest. Finally he settled on a mountaintop, with nothing but a moss-covered boulder for a pillow. He missed his barn, and he missed the Terisons.

Almost a year went by. Then, one spring day, a man came hiking up the mountain. It was Elwood Terison! Jeremy couldn't believe his eyes.

"What are you doing here?" he asked.

Elwood ran to him. "I'm so glad I've found you. After you left, a terrible storm destroyed the orchard and the bridge. My sons and daughters-in-law had no apple trees to look after. They went and got jobs in the city. Sal and I—we're the only ones left. We need your help."

"I'll come," said Jeremy.

He came down from the mountain, built another raft, and paddled hard upriver with Elwood by his side. The next morning, they reached the orchard.

Sal was there to hug them both. "Thank goodness you're back, Jeremy," she said.

Big Jeremy strode into the orchard. Uprooted apple trees were scattered everywhere.

Jeremy took a deep breath and let it go. Instantly the trees were blown into a pile in the corner of a field.

Now it was time to get to work. Jeremy plowed the earth and began planting young apple trees. In less than a day, a whole new orchard was ready to start growing.

Elwood and Sal danced around.

"You've saved us!" said Sal. "We'll have apple trees again!"

"Now I'll help with some painting," said Jeremy.

He gave the house a coat of white and the barn a coat of red. When he was through, it was still daylight.

"Now I'll fix the bridge again," he said.

He was just getting started when the shouting began on the other side of the river. It was the Terisons' seven sons and daughters-in-law and all their grandchildren. Elwood had called them in the city and told them what Jeremy had done. They wanted to come home!

Big Jeremy stretched himself between the two shores. The seven sons and daughters-in-law and all the grandchildren tried not to tickle him as they raced across his back. When they reached the other side, they cheered, and Jeremy gave all the children rides on his shoulders.

Setting the last one down on the ground, he grinned. "Now you can help me with the bridge."

When the work was done, Jeremy had a picnic supper with the entire Terison family. "It's good to be home," he said.

Then he went back to his enormous barn. He swept away the cobwebs, settled into his chair, and watched the sunset.